Ruby and Little Joe

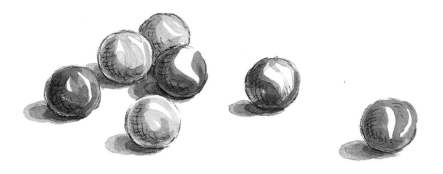

For Emilia.
— A.McA.
For Niki and Jude, with love.
— T.M.

SIMON AND SCHUSTER

First published in Great Britain in 2006 by Simon & Schuster UK Ltd

Africa House, 64-78 Kingsway, London WC2B 6AH

This paperback edition first published in 2006

Text copyright © 2006 Angela McAllister

Illustrations copyright © 2006 Terry Milne

The right of Angela McAllister and Terry Milne to be identified
as the author and illustrator of this work has been asserted by them
in accordance with the Copyright, Designs and Patents Act, 1988

Book designed by Genevieve Webster
The text for this book is set in Joanna and Bernhard Modern
The illustrations are rendered in watercolour

A CIP catalogue record for this book is available from the British Library upon request

ISBN 0-689-87243-7
Printed in China
1 3 5 7 9 10 8 6 4 2

Ruby and Little Joe

Angela McAllister & Terry Milne

SIMON AND SCHUSTER
London New York Sydney

Ruby and Little Joe arrived one day without any wrapping or ribbon.

"Which shop are you from?" asked the other toys.

"We've come from a house where the children have all grown up," said Ruby, shyly.

"You mean you're second-hand?" sneered Camel.

Little Joe tumbled out of Ruby's pouch and somersaulted across the floor. "We're tenth-hand!" he cried with a giggle.

"Well, not quite," said Ruby, patting his ears.

Camel looked down her nose at Little Joe. "You'll find everybody here is new and very fine," she said.

"Don't you get played with?" asked Little Joe.

"No. We're much too special to play with. We get admired," replied Camel.

Little Joe whispered in Ruby's ear. "Is that the same as loved?"

"No, dear," said Ruby sadly.

With a snort Camel walked off and the other toys followed.

"Oh, Mama," gasped Little Joe. "I don't like it here. Shall we run away?"

"No," said Ruby. "This is our home now. We must stay here and try to make friends. Maybe one day they will like us."

That night Ruby and Little Joe were not invited
to sleep on the end of the bed with the other toys,
so they climbed into a jigsaw box on the
toy-shelf and curled up there.

Little Joe tried hard to stay out of trouble,
but he was full of bump and tumble. The toys
got cross with him every day.

Ruby made herself useful.
She fetched dominoes for Camel,
who liked to look clever.

She carried a mirror for Monkey,
who thought he was handsome.

She collected marbles for Polar Bear.
And she carried Mouse all over
the house.

With Ruby's pouch always full there was no room for Little Joe. He tried riding on her tail but he wriggled so much he fell off.

"You're a big boy now, Little Joe," said Ruby. "You'll have to walk."

Little Joe didn't feel like a big boy but he pretended, for his mama. He even tried to be helpful, sorting bricks and beads, but still the toys wouldn't let Ruby and Little Joe sleep at the end of the bed.

One day Ruby dropped Camel's dominoes down the stairs. She had to go up and down again and again to fetch them. That night her legs were too tired to climb into the jigsaw box.

Little Joe pulled himself up onto the bed. "Please let Mama sleep here," he said. "Have a heart."

"What is a heart?" asked Mouse.

"It's what's inside you," said Little Joe awkwardly. "It's the part that cares."

"We've got the softest, most expensive stuffing inside us," said Camel. "There's nothing better than that."

"Yes there is," whispered Little Joe to himself.

Next morning Little Joe said, "I'll carry today, Mama. I'm a big boy now."

He carried marbles for Polar Bear and a doll's comb for Monkey. Then Camel called for her dominoes. Little Joe struggled. With his arms full he couldn't see where he was going. Suddenly he stepped right off the table and fell into the waste paper basket.

Moments later the bedroom door was opened and the basket taken away.

Ruby looked
everywhere for
Little Joe.
"Shouldn't we help?"
asked Mouse.
"No. It's much quieter
without him,"
scoffed Camel.

So poor Ruby searched alone for hours in the dark house. Then, as she crept across the kitchen windowsill, she suddenly heard a cry.

"Maaaaaama!"

Outside, peeping from under the dustbin lid was Little Joe.

Ruby waved but she couldn't jump down that far. So to comfort Little Joe she sat by the window all night and sang to him.

Next morning Ruby slipped through the kitchen door and out into the rain.

"Oh, Mama, I can't climb down," said Little Joe. "It's such a long way."

"I'll reach you," promised Ruby.

Ruby climbed on a brick but she couldn't reach Little Joe. She tried to push a flowerpot up to the dustbin but it was too heavy. "If only I had some help," she sighed.

Little Joe looked up and saw the toys
watching at the window.
A tear rolled down his cheek.

Mouse gave a quiet cough. "I think…" he said timidly, "I think… I want to help."

"What!" Camel snorted. "Why would you want to get wet and dirty to help a couple of hand-me-downs?"

"I think it's something to do with heart," said Mouse.

"I'll help too," said Polar Bear.

"And me," said Monkey. "Ruby fetched and carried for us, now we can help her."

"Hmmmph!" Camel huffed and puffed. "Well, of course I am the tallest. You can't reach without me!"

So, to Ruby's astonishment, Camel led the toys out to the dirty, wet dustbin. Then they climbed up onto Camel's back – Polar Bear, Monkey and last of all Mouse.

Little Joe reached down… Mouse stretched up… and pulled him out!

"Thank you!" said Ruby and Little Joe, hugging each other tight.

That night Camel herself made room for Ruby
and Little Joe to sleep on the bed. And, as all the toys
nestled together, they felt a good, warm feeling inside
their expensive stuffing. Mouse knew it was his heart.